BRINGING THE RAIN TO KAPITI PLAIN

A Nandi Tale

BRINGING THE RAIN TO KAPITI PLAIN

retold by Verna Aardema / pictures by Beatriz Vidal

PUFFIN BOOKS

PUFFIN BOOKS
Published by the Penguin Group
Penguin Putnam Books for Young Readers, 345 Hudson Street, New York, New York 10014, U.S.A.
Penguin Books Ltd, 27 Wrights Lane, London W8 5TZ, England
Penguin Books Australia Ltd, Ringwood, Victoria, Australia
Penguin Books Canada Ltd, 10 Alcorn Avenue, Toronto, Ontario, Canada M4V 3B2
Penguin Books (N.Z.) Ltd, 182-190 Wairau Road, Auckland 10, New Zealand

Penguin Books Ltd, Registered Offices: Harmondsworth, Middlesex, England

First published by Dial Books for Young Readers, a division of Penguin Books USA Inc., 1981
First published by Puffin Books, 1983
40

ISBN 0-14-054616-2
LIBRARY OF CONGRESS CATALOG CARD NUMBER: 80-25886

Printed in U.S.A.

For my librarian,
Bernice Houseward
V. A.

For my parents; for my teacher
B. V.

This is the great
    Kapiti Plain,
All fresh and green
    from the African rains—
A sea of grass for the
    ground birds to nest in,
And patches of shade for
    wild creatures to rest in;
With acacia trees for
    giraffes to browse on,
And grass for the herdsmen
    to pasture their cows on.

But one year the rains
    were so very belated,
That all of the big wild
    creatures migrated.
Then Ki-pat helped to end
    that terrible drought—
And this story tells
    how it all came about!

This is the cloud,
all heavy with rain,
That shadowed the ground
on Kapiti Plain.

This is the grass,
    all brown and dead,
That needed the rain
    from the cloud overhead—
The big, black cloud,
    all heavy with rain,
That shadowed the ground
    on Kapiti Plain.

These are the cows,
    all hungry and dry,
Who mooed for the rain
    to fall from the sky;
To green-up the grass,
    all brown and dead,
That needed the rain
    from the cloud overhead—
The big, black cloud,
    all heavy with rain,
That shadowed the ground
    on Kapiti Plain.

This is Ki-pat,
   who watched his herd
As he stood on one leg,
   like the big stork bird;
Ki-pat, whose cows
   were so hungry and dry,
They mooed for the rain
   to fall from the sky;
To green-up the grass,
   all brown and dead,
That needed the rain
   from the cloud overhead—
The big, black cloud,
   all heavy with rain,
That shadowed the ground
   on Kapiti Plain.

This is the eagle
    who dropped a feather,
A feather that helped
    to change the weather.
It fell near Ki-pat,
    who watched his herd
As he stood on one leg,
    like the big stork bird;
Ki-pat, whose cows
    were so hungry and dry,
They mooed for the rain
    to fall from the sky;
To green-up the grass,
    all brown and dead,
That needed the rain
    from the cloud overhead—
The big, black cloud,
    all heavy with rain,
That shadowed the ground
    on Kapiti Plain.

This is the arrow
    Ki-pat put together,
With a slender stick
    and an eagle feather;
From the eagle who happened
    to drop a feather,
A feather that helped
    to change the weather.

It fell near Ki-pat,
      who watched his herd
As he stood on one leg,
      like the big stork bird;
Ki-pat, whose cows
      were so hungry and dry,
They mooed for the rain
      to fall from the sky;
To green-up the grass,
      all brown and dead,
That needed the rain
      from the cloud overhead—
The big, black cloud,
      all heavy with rain,
That shadowed the ground
      on Kapiti Plain.

This is the bow,
    so long and strong,
And strung with a string,
    a leather thong;
A bow for the arrow
    Ki-pat put together,
With a slender stick
    and an eagle feather;
From the eagle who happened
    to drop a feather,
A feather that helped
    to change the weather.

It fell near Ki-pat,
  who watched his herd
As he stood on one leg,
  like the big stork bird;
Ki-pat, whose cows
  were so hungry and dry,
They mooed for the rain
  to fall from the sky;
To green-up the grass,
  all brown and dead,
That needed the rain
  from the cloud overhead—
The big, black cloud,
  all heavy with rain,
That shadowed the ground
  on Kapiti Plain.

This was the shot
   that pierced the cloud
And loosed the rain
   with thunder LOUD!
A shot from the bow,
   so long and strong,
And strung with a string,
   a leather thong;
A bow for the arrow
   Ki-pat put together,
With a slender stick
   and an eagle feather;
From the eagle who happened
   to drop a feather,
A feather that helped
   to change the weather.

It fell near Ki-pat,
    who watched his herd
As he stood on one leg,
    like the big stork bird;
Ki-pat, whose cows
    were so hungry and dry,
They mooed for the rain
    to fall from the sky;
To green-up the grass,
    all brown and dead,
That needed the rain
    from the cloud overhead—
The big, black cloud,
    all heavy with rain,
That shadowed the ground
    on Kapiti Plain.

So the grass grew green,
and the cattle fat!
And Ki-pat got a wife
and a little Ki-pat—

Who tends the cows now,
 and shoots down the rain,
When black clouds shadow
 Kapiti Plain.